Hey Diddle Diddle

Story by:
Michelle Baron

Illustrated by:

Theresa Mazurek   Rivka
Douglas McCarthy   Fay Whitemountain
Allyn Conley-Gorniak   Su-Zan
Lorann Downer   Lisa Souza

This Book Belongs To:

Use this symbol to match book and cassette.

This nursery rhyme is called "Hey, Diddle, Diddle." It will help us learn about imagination.

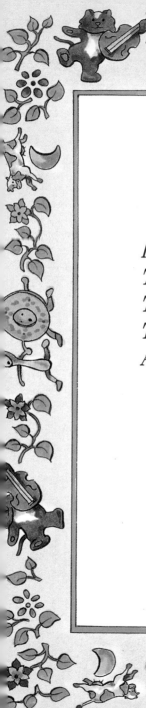

Hey, diddle, diddle,
The cat and the fiddle,
The cow jumped over the moon.
The little dog laughed to see such sport
And the dish ran away with the spoon.

Hector didn't think he had an imagination. So he went out onto the porch
to see if he could get one. Hector sat
for a long time. After a while we met
on the porch.

Then Hector told me a most wonderful
story.

"I was sitting on the porch steps for a long, long time, doing nothing. Then that funny nursery rhyme popped into my head and all of a sudden a big cow almost backed right into me!

The cow was going to jump to the moon, and she needed a big running start.

It takes a lot of energy to jump that far!

The cow had to hurry because it was almost noon.

She had to be on the moon at noon.

I've always wondered what it was really like on the moon.

So, I climbed up onto the back of the cow.

We started running. We ran faster and faster, and we jumped up into the sky.

We went real, real high until I couldn't
see the house anymore. Then it got
very dark.

I could see the stars. It was beautiful.

I saw constellations!

One was called the "Big Dipper."

It was a fast ride and soon we were on the moon.

It was big and it talked to me.

The moon was very nice, and we talked for a long time. He told me that it was cold living in space.

Then a rocket ship landed, and a cat with a fiddle, a little dog, and a dish and a spoon got out.

Then they started setting up a table.

I asked them what they were doing, and they said it was time for tea!

They have tea on the moon every day at noon!

''Tea On The Moon''

Tea on the moon every day at noon,
The dish and the spoon dance to a tune
That's played by a fiddler cat.
It's something to see,
And we sing off-key in harmony!
Tea with me,
Have some tea with me.

We try very hard to be neat and polite.
You don't look very neat to me.
He's right!
The spoon tries to stir everybody's tea.
They're a very bad-mannered menagerie.

Tea on the moon every day at noon,
The dish and the spoon dance to a tune
That's played by a fiddler cat.
It's something to see,
And we sing off-key in harmony!
Tea with me,
Have some tea with me.

So, this is what happened. The cow, the dish and the spoon, and the cat and the dog all sat down to have their tea. Well, they were very quiet and polite at first, but that didn't last long!

They reached for the food at the same time, and they all got in each other's way. And boy, were they noisy! Then, all of a sudden, they got up and started dancing!

Song Continued

*They go into their dance and the cow starts
    to hop,
Then all of the food starts to drop.
The dish and the spoon are spinning 'round
    like a top!
Will somebody go out and get me a mop?*

*Tea on the moon every day at noon,
The dish and the spoon dance to a tune
That's played by a fiddler cat.
It's something to see,
And we sing off-key in harmony!
Tea with me,
Have some tea with me.*

We had lots of fun together. After tea, the cat and the fiddle, the little dog, the dish and the spoon, and the cow cleaned up and put everything away. And I helped them!

Then I got back on the cow and we jumped all the way down.

And here I am!"

That was a wonderful story Hector told, wasn't it?

And it took a lot of imagination.

So it didn't take long for Hector to realize that he really had an imagination after all. When he did, he was very excited.

You see, everyone has an imagination. Imagining comes easily.

''Imagining Comes Easily''

Chorus

Imagining comes easily,
Just close your eyes and find
The world that's waiting there for you
Right inside your mind.
Imagining comes easily.
Just close your eyes and see
The far-off places you can go
Though you'll still be here with me.

New things, old things,
Big things and small,
Fat things, thin things,
Short things and tall,
They're yours if you want them,
Yours if you call.
You can be anyone or anywhere.
You can be anything at all!

Repeat Chorus